It turned out that Trish and Bridget and I had four classes together. I soon learned that they were two of the most popular girls in school, among the "regs," that is. All the guys waved at them. And each time someone stopped to talk, Trish or Bridget introduced me.

By the time I got to my last period drama class, I was really beginning to enjoy my new school and my new friends. It had been a long time since anyone had bothered to get to know me, especially popular kids. I wasn't sure why I had been so lucky this time, but I didn't care. And I wasn't going to do or say anything to ruin it.

the popularity
SECRET

by Cindy Savage

To my adoptive family at Mabel Gillis Library, where inspiration goes hand in hand with love

Cover photo by John Strange

Published by Willowisp Press, Inc.
10100 SBF Drive, Pinellas Park, Florida 34666

Printed in the United States of America

10 9 8 7 6 5 4

ISBN 0-87406-315-9

One

"BUT I don't want to move again," I complained. I didn't want to sound whiny, but this was the fifth move in less than two years. "Where to this time?" I asked. "Not another apartment, I hope."

Mrs. Shelley, my placement worker, smiled. "I know it has been difficult for you these last two years since your adoptive parents died, Janet. I know you've been on the foster home merry-go-round waiting for the right family to come along and give you a permanent home. Let's face it. It's difficult to find a family willing to take on a teenager."

I sighed and dropped my chin into my hands, my elbows resting on my knees. What was wrong with me that no one wanted to give me a home for longer than a few months? I wasn't a troublemaker. I liked school. I didn't smart-mouth my foster parents.

But so far I hadn't been good enough for anybody's family. Mrs. Shelley always told me to be patient and wait. The right family would come along. I wasn't so sure that this family would turn out to be the one we'd been waiting for either.

If only my parents hadn't died in that stupid car crash. Everything had been so great. We had a beautiful house with a swimming pool and a sheepdog. I had lots of friends, and my parents and I did everything together. It seemed like forever since I'd had someone to talk to and do things with.

"You'll like the Kingsleys," Mrs. Shelley said. She wrote some things down in her notebook. I'd long since given up trying to figure out what people were writing down about me. It didn't matter, anyway. As long as I was under 18, the county had control over my life. I couldn't even find out who my real mother and father were until then.

As long as I'd lived with the Martins, I'd never wondered who my real parents were. It didn't matter, because the Martins had adopted me when I was a baby. They were the only parents I'd ever known. But the last two years of home-shopping had given me plenty of time to think about the people who gave me up in the beginning.

The place where I was living now was awful. There were so many rules. "Janet, do the laundry." "Janet, watch the twins." I had to cook dinner, do the dishes, and wash the car. I couldn't talk on the phone for more than five minutes at a time. I had to do my homework the minute I got home from school. No snacks. No friends over. No fun.

On top of all the rules and chores, the Davises always complained. Mrs. Davis' favorite line was, "The girl is going to eat us out of house and home. The county doesn't pay enough for all the trouble she causes."

Mrs. Davis didn't feel that way about the babies though. Her twins were her life. I figured that the Davis family had only agreed to take me because they needed a baby-sitter.

"I think you'll like living on a small farm in the country after being in that cramped apartment." Mrs. Shelley's voice broke into my thoughts. "Do you like animals? I hear the Kingsleys raise and show sheep at the fair."

My eyes lit up. "I do like animals. We used to have a sheepdog named Alfred. He slept with me when I was sick. Mom and Dad didn't mind. He slept with them sometimes, too."

Mrs. Shelley laughed, and I laughed, too. "Well, then, this seems like it might be the right place for you. The last time I was there

Mr. Kingsley was showing me a new litter of puppies and some newborn pigmy goats. All the children have their own special pets."

This was sounding too good to be true, but I wasn't going to get my hopes up yet. At the apartment house I couldn't even talk the Davises into a goldfish.

"Is there anything special I should do to make them like me?" I asked. "Everywhere else I stayed, I always did something to make them not like me. I left my bed unmade, or I brought home too many colds from school and made their kids sick."

Mrs. Shelley smiled and laid her hand on my shoulder. "You haven't done anything wrong, Janet. I admit you've seen your share of temporary homes. The Browns got transferred to another state. The Philips had a baby of their own. The Davises decided they wanted to tour Europe without school-age children to worry about. None of those things were your fault. Those homes were just short-term while we tried to find you an adoptive family. Now I hope we've found one. I'll tell you a secret." She leaned close. "The Kingsleys are very wonderful people, and I've never seen them send anyone back."

"No matter what?" I asked.

"No matter what," she said.

Two

THE end of September crackled with heat. Mrs. Shelley's car didn't have air conditioning, but I didn't care. I loved the feel of the hot wind blowing through my hair and drying the tears on my face.

I don't know why I cried. It wasn't that I would miss the Davises. And I knew they wouldn't miss me. Mrs. Davis made me do all my chores as usual this morning, and then she helped me pack my suitcase. She'd only let me take one dress, one pair of pants, and two blouses with me.

All my other things she made me leave in the closet for the next child. She kept all the clothes, she said, because she never knew who the county was going to send her next, after her trip to Europe, of course. I thought she wasn't going to take any more older kids, but I didn't say anything. Obviously, the Davises simply didn't want me to live with them.

I was glad to leave. I just hated going to a new home looking like what I was, an orphan. I wondered if the new home would have a stack of clothes that would fit me left over from the last child.

Two cows stood lazily chewing their cuds behind a split-rail fence. They raised their heads as we drove by.

We passed fields of corn and alfalfa. And we saw horses grazing and sheep drinking from shallow water holes. There were few houses until we rounded a small hill. Then I saw a large sign that said Sheldon Hills Estates.

"Here we are," Mrs. Shelley announced as we drove through two brick gateposts and into a development of homes. Each house sat on a few acres of land. We wound around through the paved streets and finally turned into a long gravel driveway.

A tall lady in jeans and a blue and white striped T-shirt stood up from the garden as we drove in. She wiped her hands on her pants and walked over to where Mrs. Shelley parked the car.

"Well, here you are at last!" She beamed her welcome in the window at me. "Mrs. Shelley," she said to my placement worker, "it's so nice to see you again. Let's get Janet settled, and then I hope you'll stay for lunch."

The lady stuck out her hand to me, and we shook. "I'm Sherry Kingsley," she said, introducing herself. "But everyone around here calls me Mom—even all the kids in the neighborhood. You can, too, if you like."

Mrs. Kingsley was a lot younger than all my other foster mothers. She had blond, sun-streaked hair that was pulled back into a high ponytail. She smelled like fresh air and hay, and she was wearing high-tops.

"Is that all they sent with you?" she asked, clicking her tongue and eyeing my small suitcase.

"Y—Yes," I stammered. "I'm sorry." I looked down at my feet where my toes were threatening to poke out of my cheap, discount-store tennis shoes. Mrs. Davis was always complaining about how fast I grew out of shoes. I looked up to apologize again, but Mrs. Kingsley wasn't frowning.

"No matter, honey. I'm sure I can whip you up a couple of nice outfits for school. And if you don't mind hand-me-downs, I think Rosemary is about your size."

"I don't mind," I told her. "Who's Rosemary?"

"She's my daughter. She was a foster child just like you when she came five years ago.

But she's ours now, and it's wonderful to have her. She and Francis are going to be your roommates," Mrs. Kingsley went on to explain. "Come on. I'll introduce you to the gang."

She bustled us up the stairs, through the massive, carved wooden doors, and into the entryway. Everywhere I looked there were umbrellas and coats on hooks. Rubber boots and work boots were lined up in rows along the wall. A pair of crutches leaned against a folded wheelchair.

I started to ask about the crutches and wheelchair, but suddenly we heard a loud crash from around the corner. Everything was quiet for a few seconds, and then the shouting started.

I looked at Mrs. Kingsley in surprise.

"I hope you like noise," she said, laughing. "We love each other around here, but we sure are loud."

Mrs. Shelley smiled, and we followed my new foster mother into the kitchen.

"It was your fault," shouted a small boy bracing himself on a silver cane with a wrist strap. "You shouldn't have been carrying the bowl in the first place."

"How was I to know you'd trip me with your cane?" a tall, dark-haired girl asked loudly. "In case you have to be reminded, I can't see, you know."

"It would be nice if you couldn't talk, too," said another boy, seated at the table in a wheelchair. "I can't concentrate on putting this model together with all the shouting that goes on around here."

"It doesn't help even if you can't hear," spoke a blond-headed boy in a flat tone. "The vibrations alone would kill you."

Mrs. Kingsley stood at the doorway with her hands on her hips, surveying the scene. "Are you all finished?" she asked quietly. "I'd like you to meet your new sister."

Five faces turned toward her and tried to peer around through the doorway at me. "Group," she said, "meet Janet, the newest member of the Kingsley household. I want you to make her welcome, which means not acting like you usually do. Try to hold it down a little, okay?"

"Hi, Janet!" everyone shouted at once.

"Rosemary," Mrs. Kingsley said to a girl about my age on the other side of the big oak table, "will you introduce your brothers and sisters while I find out from Francis what happened with the mixing bowl?"

"Sure, Mom. Hi, I'm Rosemary." She came around the table to stand by me. "I'm in seventh grade, the same as you are. This is Biff." She pointed at the boy who had said he couldn't hear. "He's a grade ahead of us at Sheldon School. And this is Jones." She introduced me to a small black boy with a cane.

I barely listened to what she said. I was too busy trying not to look at his arm. Where his hand should have been, he had a shiny, metal, robotlike arm.

"It's okay, Janet. Everyone stares at first," he said and grinned. "I have fake legs, too." He pulled up his cuffs to show me. "I was born without legs."

"Oh," was all I could manage to say. "Does it hurt?" I squeaked out, and then wished I had kept my mouth shut. I closed my eyes tightly and opened them again, but no one was staring at me like I thought they would be.

"Not usually. Want to see how they work?" he asked. Jones pushed his sleeve up with his good hand and showed me the plastic arm-shaped piece attached to the hook. It was dark to match his skin. "See this cable that goes up my arm and across my back? It works the hook so I can open and close it." He snapped the hook at my nose.

I jumped about a foot and swallowed hard. "That's really neat," I said, without much enthusiasm. I tried to smile.

"Want to see how the legs work?" He was already rolling up his pants legs. I wished Rosemary would get on with the introductions. I wanted to get away from Jones. I'd never been in the same room with so many handicapped people in my life, and I felt a little suffocated.

"This is James," Rosemary said, pointing to a boy in a wheelchair. "He's in fifth grade. Jones is in sixth," she added as she shoved his snapping hook out of our way.

The blind girl's name was Francis. She was in tenth grade. She was still talking to Mrs. Kingsley about the mixing bowl.

"What's wrong with you?" James rolled his wheelchair over to where I was standing and looked up at me.

"Well . . . I . . ."

A big, muscular man in denim overalls came to my rescue. "Janet's only handicap is having to listen to you guys," he boomed. "After all this commotion she probably wishes she could turn right around and run."

That was for sure.

"Hi!" He stuck out his big hand and shook mine thoroughly. "I'm Bob Kingsley, Pop around here." He continued pumping my hand. Mr. and Mrs. Kingsley didn't look at all like any other parents I'd been sent to.

"Pop," Jones yelled, "you're going to shake her arm off, and I don't have any extras."

"Hold your voice down, and stop teasing Janet," Mr. Kingsley finally dropped my hand. He gave Jones a gentle punch on his good shoulder. "Watch out for this guy!" he warned me. Then he greeted Mrs. Shelley and headed back outside.

"A farmer's work is never done," he said on his way out the door.

"Oh, pooh!" Mrs. Kingsley laughed. "Pop is trying to hand you a line. He's only a farmer on the weekends. The rest of the time he's a computer programmer in town."

"Caught again," he called back over his shoulder. "See you at lunch, Janet."

"You will if she doesn't get eaten first," Jones said, hobbling past me and snapping his hook as he went.

"Don't pay any attention to his scare tactics." Mrs. Kingsley laughed again. "Well, I never said it was calm around here," she added when she saw my strickened look. "Rosemary is going to show you the bathroom and the bedroom you'll share with Francis and her. Then we're going to have lunch. Off you go," she said, waving us down the hallway.

"Janet." Mrs. Shelley put her hand on my

shoulder. "I'm not going to be able to stay for lunch, but I'm sure you're in good hands."

"But . . ." I didn't go on. I knew my eyes were pleading with her not to leave me here all alone. I wasn't like these kids. Rosemary appeared to be the only normal kid here besides me. And I wasn't sure about her yet. *Why would the county make me live here, of all places?*

"I'll be in touch," Mrs. Shelley called back as she headed for her car.

I swallowed again, hoping the lump in my throat would go away. The kids all seemed nice enough, but I didn't think I could handle being around them all the time. Rosemary showed me around and explained the chore chart and what I had to do to earn my keep.

Why me? I thought over and over as I followed Rosemary back down the extra-wide hallway and into the kitchen. *Why me?*

Three

THE weekend flew by. Saturday I was whisked away to the department store with Mrs. Kingsley. She wanted to buy me some clothes for school. She told me to choose what I wanted. She handed me dresses, skirts, jeans, tops, and coats to try on. I tried to look at the expressions on her face to see which ones she wanted me to pick. But she just smiled and nodded and told me I had to choose, because I was going to be the one to wear them.

All the clothes were nice. But I knew I'd better not choose too many. I didn't want to seem greedy. Mrs. Davis' voice came back to me as I studied the clothes. *They give me money to feed and clothe you, not for you to prance around like some fancy movie star!*

Then again I didn't want to choose too few. I could tell by the way Mrs. Kingsley kept handing me things to try on that she would be hurt if I only bought one thing.

My head pounded as I tried to figure out the answer. I finally held up a pair of light blue jeans, a denim skirt and two blouses.

"Is that all you want, hon?" Mrs. Kingsley asked.

I looked down. I knew I would do the wrong thing. I thought I was being thrifty, but it didn't work.

"Honey"—she took my chin in her warm hand and lifted it so I could see her face—"I didn't realize you'd have such a hard time deciding. Well, let me show you what I 've seen the kids at school wear, and we'll choose together."

"Thanks," I said softly. "I just wasn't sure—a new place and all, you know."

A twinkle lit her eyes, and a dimple appeared in her cheek. She put her arm around me, and it felt nice, like it was supposed to be there.

"Now let's see." She continued grinning. "If I were in junior high and wanted to make a good impression on my first day of school, I'd wear . . ." She shuffled through the rack and brought out a turquoise sweater and a shirt with the same color of turquoise in it. Then she added a skirt.

"Those look great together." I sighed, knowing that the outfit was probably too expensive.

"And look," she said, pulling a similar outfit off the rack. This one had peachy tones. "They'll mix and match, and you'll have six outfits instead of two."

By the time we'd left the store, I was carrying two huge bags and a smaller plastic one with underwear and socks. Mrs. Kingsley had my two new pairs of shoes. I couldn't believe it. I wondered if I'd have to work twice as hard to pay her back for all these things.

Later that afternoon, Rosemary was admiring my clothes as I hung them in our closet.

She described the colors and styles to Francis, who was sitting on her bed reading a braille novel. Francis put down her book to come over and feel the fabric.

"Nice," Francis said. She smiled, but her eyes just stared at me, and they flickered a little. I looked away, trying not to stare back.

"Did Mom stop by the fabric store?" Francis asked casually.

"Uh huh." I tried to sound normal. "She bought some green striped material and some gray wool. She didn't say what for, though."

"Well, I know she's making Jones a shirt out of the green," Rosemary said. "She has to make all of his clothes so the straps and buckles on his legs and arm don't show."

"Tell me about the school," I said to change the subject. I didn't want to talk about handicaps anymore.

"Sheldon School is a special school," Rosemary said as she helped me find a place for my shoes. "A lot of handicapped kids go there. It's a mainstreaming program."

"What does mainstreaming mean?"

Francis settled back down to her book and let Rosemary explain. "They want handicapped kids to get along in the 'mainstream' of society. So the school has special classes to teach living skills, like balancing checkbooks, cooking—even eating and getting in and out of cars and stuff like that. And since the school is out in the country, there's also a program where kids can learn about animals on the school farm."

"Do all of you go to the same school?" I asked, thinking that Jones and James were in elementary school.

"Yep. Kindergarten through senior high go to the same school. And besides the kids who live in Sheldon Hills, others are bussed from three towns because the programs in the school are so good."

I folded my socks and placed them side by side in the top drawer of the dresser. Then I neatly folded my new underwear and laid them next to the socks. One of my other foster mothers had taught me to keep my drawers neat at all times. According to her a neat person was a nice person. I wasn't taking any chances here.

"Do you like the school? Do you have a lot of friends?" I asked Rosemary.

She hesitated a minute, then brushed her bangs out of her eyes. "Yes," she said finally. "I have a few friends."

"I hope I make some friends, too," I said.

"I'm sure you will, Janet," Rosemary said. But she looked worried. I couldn't understand why.

* * * * *

Breakfast at the Kingsley household was pretty wild. Mr. Kingsley looked like a short-order cook as he slapped pancakes on our plates. Mrs. Kingsley poured the juice and milk. "Hurry up, kids. You'll miss the bus!"

We all had to catch the bus at the same time. Rosemary explained that most of the kids in the neighborhood had to walk the mile to school, but the Kingsleys had their own special bus.

"You're going to really like Sheldon school,"

James told me as he wheeled his chair past the line of sack lunches and grabbed the one with his name on it. "We play basketball and swim and help bottle-feed the baby goats."

"Okay, James." Francis came up behind him and gave his chair a push. "You'll talk all day, and we really will miss the bus." As she pushed him, he reached up and gently pressed his fingers into one side of her hand or the other to tell her which way to go. If I hadn't been looking, I probably wouldn't have noticed it. In fact, I probably wouldn't have even known Francis was blind. She seemed so sure of herself. I wished I felt as confident about my first day at yet another new school. I really wanted people to like me. I wanted to make some friends and get into some activities.

"Don't forget your lunch," Biff reminded me.

"Thanks," I said, and turned to pick up the sack. "I'm used to making my own lunch. I didn't—"

I felt a hand on my shoulder and turned back around to see Biff looking at me with a grin on his face. "Did you say something?" he asked politely.

My face turned red. "I'm sorry, Biff. I forgot I had to talk straight at you."

"It's okay," he said, his grin growing wider.

"I just like to read those cute lips of yours. Come on." He pulled me outside by the hand. "I'll walk you to the bus."

Mrs. Kingsley watched us as we left. I waved, but didn't look at her. I didn't want to see the expression on her face. She probably thought I was stupid. I made so many mistakes.

I shook my hand free from Biff's and walked a little behind him out to the small golden school bus. I didn't want him to see me wipe off the tear that tried to escape. *Why didn't I remember that Biff was deaf? Oh, why can't I do something right for a change?*

Four

THERE were no other kids on the special bus, just the Kingsley family and me. We took up all the seats.

Francis stared blankly out the window.

"She's moping about Saul Blackwell. She's in luuvv," James cooed.

Francis turned back toward James with a scowl on her face.

"Is Saul your boyfriend?" I asked.

"No," she grumbled. "And I don't want to talk about it!"

"Boy, you're a grouch today!" James complained. "Don't yell at Janet. She doesn't know how many times you've hoped that Saul Blackwell would ask you out. You know he's a lost cause."

"Oooh, you're impossible!" Francis said.

"I'm supposed to be impossible. I'm 10 years old," James said, sticking his tongue out at her and crossing his eyes.

"Hush, James." Rosemary put her hand on his arm. "When you're older, I'm sure you'll understand."

I clenched my hands in my lap. *It's bad enough trying to make friends when you're new,* I thought. *What if I were blind?*

The small, yellow bus pulled up in front of a group of flat, colorful buildings. In fact, I'd never seen a school so brightly painted.

"Well, thank goodness we're finally here," Francis snarled. She grasped the handrails and stomped down the wide steps of the bus. "Now you guys can stop talking about me."

As we entered the building, I wondered who Saul Blackwell was. Just talking about him seemed to make Francis mad.

Rosemary led the way past walls of painted murals. Some of the scenes were wild. On one wall, even the window frames and shades were blue to match the sky scene that was painted all around them. Across the top of the wall, almost to the ceiling, a single jet flew. Its silver body trailed plumes of white vapor trails.

"Wow, that painting is beautiful!" I exclaimed.

"The artist goes to school here," Rosemary said proudly. She looked past the jet in flight to a series of abstract portraits of mythical gods and goddesses. Their hair and clothes mingled and fluttered in an unseen breeze. "His name is David Williams. He did this whole corridor last year. He's really good, isn't he?"

"I'll say." I continued admiring the murals until we reached the office.

"See you at lunch or on the bus later," Rosemary called as she headed down the hall.

I waved and then turned to the lady behind the desk. "I'm Janet Martin," I said. "Do you have my schedule?"

"Mrs. Kingsley said we should expect you today," she told me. She looked over my records. "Glad to have you with us. Follow me." She wheeled herself out from behind the huge desk. "I'll take you to your first class."

Boy, even the office workers are handicapped. I followed her up and down the ramps to the portable buildings in the back of the school. *This is going to take some getting used to,* I thought to myself. I was beginning to feel really out of place because I could walk, talk, see, and hear. I wished I was as calm about being here as Rosemary was. Maybe she was used to seeing handicapped people, but I wasn't.

I had science first period. The teacher introduced me to the class, and I sank into a seat on the left side of the room. I tried to concentrate on the diagram of a water molecule the teacher was drawing on the board. But I felt people looking at me. I always hate the first day in a new school.

After class a blond-haired girl came up to me. "Hi!" she said. "I'm Trish. Are you a reg or a crip?"

"What? I'm sorry . . ." I stammered. "I don't understand."

"Never mind. I can tell you're a reg. Regular," she explained. "You know, not handicapped."

"Oh." I smiled. "No, I'm not handicapped."

"I just wondered," she said. "I saw you get off the bus with all those retard Kingsley kids."

"Don't you like them?" I asked carefully.

"We just don't mix, that's all." She raised her books higher on her hip and asked me where my next class was.

I looked at the computer printout of my schedule. "I have P.E.," I told her.

"Great!" she said. "So do I. I can introduce you to Bridget."

Trish was off in a flash. I practically had to run to catch up. I followed her into the locker room and handed my new-student form to the teacher.

"Change anywhere and leave your clothes in one of the lockers," the teacher said. "Here's an extra gym outfit. You'll have to buy your own by next week." She handed me a pair of blue shorts and a white T-shirt. "Trish," she said, "you and Bridget show her the routine. Let's go, ladies," she shouted. "Everybody outside for exercises."

Trish and Bridget found me a locker near theirs. It was right in the center of a bunch of regular girls in great-looking clothes.

I glanced around the room as I took off my peach outfit. I tried to get changed as quickly as possible. Undressing in front of people made me uncomfortable. I felt like everyone was staring at me, trying to find out if I was a reg or a crip.

I only saw two girls in wheelchairs head out to the blacktop with us. They each had on shorts and a top like mine. I wondered how they managed to dress themselves. I noticed a couple of other girls. One walked a little jerky, and the other one had someone leading her. I figured she was probably blind like Francis.

I shuddered and thought about how lucky I was not to be handicapped.

"Don't let them bug you." Bridget leaned toward me as we were stretching. "If you just ignore them, after a while you really don't even notice they're around."

How could you ignore half the school? I wondered.

"I don't know why they had to let all those retards into our school," Trish said. "By the way, you never did tell me why you rode in on the handicapped bus this morning."

"Well, I just moved to Sheldon Hills," I said. *Should I tell them I live with the Kingsleys?* I wondered.

"Oh, so you live on the same block and just thought it would be convenient?"

I knew I should tell them I lived with the Kingsleys, but I couldn't bring myself to say the words. "Yeah," I agreed. "It was the easiest thing to do until I know my way around."

"So you'll be walking tomorrow then?" Bridget asked.

"I guess so. Yeah," I told her. "I'll be walking from now on."

It turned out that Trish and Bridget and I had four classes together. I soon learned that they were two of the most popular girls in school, among the regs that is. All the boys waved at them. And each time someone stopped to talk, Trish or Bridget introduced me.

By the time I got to my last period drama

class, I was really beginning to enjoy my new school and my new friends. It had been a long time since anyone had bothered to get to know me, especially popular kids. I wasn't sure why I had been so lucky this time, but I didn't care. And I wasn't going to do or say anything to ruin it.

I was glad they had a drama class at Sheldon. My parents had let me join a children's theatre company when I was younger. I really liked it and had wanted to be involved in another play ever since.

The teacher had long gray hair and a gray beard that touched his chest. His name was Wolfgang Schmidt. Trish introduced me. He swept his arm low and bowed.

" 'Tis a fine day indeed when a new lady enters my kingdom. Dost milady favor an old knight with her dainty hand?" he clipped in old English.

"Milord," I answered to his astonishment in the same clipped tones. " 'Tis an honor. Where wouldst thou bidst me sit?"

He threw back his head and laughed, a rich, deep, well-projected sound. "Methinks I have a fair maiden to grace my court."

I curtsied, enjoying the act. "Your pleasure, sire." I made sure to look at the ground and hold my head down for a few seconds before I gazed up at Mr. Schmidt.

He clapped his hands and declared to the class, "A finer performance I have not been shown this day. Pray damoiselle, join us in our play?"

"Is he always like this?" I whispered to a stocky guy wearing a black shirt that matched his hair.

"Every day it's something new and someone new. You never know when he's going to trap you into doing a scene like that in front of the class. You were very good. Where did you learn to talk like that?"

"I was in Children's Theatre, and we did a play once about old-time England. And I've spent a lot of time at the Renaissance Faire," I told him. "My name is Janet Martin, by the way. What's yours?"

"Ah, Janet, another veteran of the stage," he said softly. "Me, too. I've done productions since I was five years old. The name's Roman Russell." He gave me a little salute as he answered my question. "But all my friends call me Rad."

Mr. Schmidt banged a tall shepherd's crook on the wooden stage to get our attention. Then he proceeded to assign groups of students to various tasks. As the other kids scrambled into line-reading groups, dance groups, and set-designing groups, he came over to me.

He handed me a script and showed me a part. It wasn't very big, but all the other parts had already been assigned, he explained. "I'll pick out a part for you to understudy later," he told me.

"You'll need to practice your lines at home tonight to catch up. You can work with a partner during class tomorrow," he added. "Everyone in my drama class works backstage, too," he explained. "Today I'd like you to choose whether you would like to do lighting, makeup, or props and scenery. Walk around and meet the kids. Then tell me what you prefer at the beginning of class tomorrow."

I wandered behind the curtain to see what went on backstage. Huge wooden cutouts in the shapes of houses and mountains were propped up against the back wall. Some were already painted, and others were still bare wood.

A guy with blond hair sat in front of one half-finished snow-capped peak. I watched as he dipped his brush into a can of white paint and quickly rubbed it sideways across the tip of the mountain. He continued dipping and swiping until the mountain was finished only minutes later.

"Wow," I exclaimed. "You're very good.

I've never seen anyone make a plain piece of wood look like a mountain so fast."

I waited for him to answer, but he just sat there.

I tried again. "Did you do all those today?" I asked, pointing to the stack of three similar mountain peaks lined up along the wall.

He still didn't answer.

Finally, he stood and picked up the mountain he'd been working on. He was careful not to touch the wet paint as he carried it over to stand beside the others. When he turned around, he looked at me and smiled.

I smiled back and stepped a little closer. "I really like your work. Have you painted for a long time?" I asked him. He seemed nice enough. Maybe he hadn't heard me before.

His forehead wrinkled into a slight frown as he shook his head. He pointed to his ears. He motioned me closer with his hands and shook his head again.

Then I saw the hearing aids and the puzzled look on his face. He was deaf. I should have thought of that.

I still wanted to tell him what I thought of his artwork. So I stepped closer and looked up into his face. As I repeated my earlier comments, I spoke loudly and slowly so he could read my lips.

He nodded his head in thanks and smiled again. I just kept staring at him. He was really cute.

"I'm Janet Martin," I told him. "What's your name?"

He took a piece of paper out of his pocket and wrote "David Williams" on it. We smiled again.

He was the guy who had painted the walls by the office. I didn't have to wander around anymore looking at makeup and lights. I decided right then that my backstage duty was going to be props and scenery.

"I saw your murals by . . ." I began. But the bell cut me off.

"Hey, Janet!" Trish poked her head around the curtain. "You'll miss your bus." She said "bus" with a baby voice.

"I have to go," I mouthed before I turned to leave. "See you tomorrow."

I grabbed my books and waved to David. As he waved back, Trish said, "Making friends with another crip, I see. Better watch out, it'll rub off on you."

"That's ridiculous," I told her. "You can't catch deafness from someone." At least I didn't think you could.

"Just remember," she said as I boarded the bus to ride home. "Crips and regs don't mix."

Five

"WOW," I said as I plopped down next to Rosemary on the narrow bus seat. "What a day! This was the best first day I ever had at a new school."

"I saw you talking to Trish. Janet . . ." Rosemary began.

"Yeah. Isn't it great? She and Bridget introduced me to all the popular kids, and they all seemed to like me. And I loved my drama class."

"That's great," Rosemary said. But I'd noticed an edge to her voice. She shifted her books. "I missed you at lunch today," she said.

"I'm sorry, Rosemary. I was coming over to sit with you and Biff when Bridget stopped me. I ended up at a table with a bunch of jocks. You know," I admitted, "I've always wondered what it would be like to be friends with the popular kids in the school."

"Trish *is* very popular," Rosemary told me quietly.

The tone of her voice made me look at her. "Hey, Rosemary, why aren't you friends with that group?" I asked.

She stared out her window. "I'm too busy with my own friends."

I didn't know what she meant exactly, but it was clear that she and Trish didn't get along. I wasn't sure why. Rosemary was a reg, too.

* * * * *

If breakfast was crazy at the Kingsley house, then dinner was an event. Mrs. Kingsley piled the table with huge platters of steaming vegetables that had been grown in the family garden and bowls full of baked potatoes and rolls.

I watched what the others were doing before I served myself. It pays not to be too quick. I remembered that from another foster family I'd lived with. The mother there served my portions so I wouldn't take too much.

I knew the Kingsleys expected me to serve myself, but I still waited a while to be sure. Finally I took a potato. I split it open the way the others had and piled the hot vegetables on it. Biff passed me the cheese sauce to pour over the top and bacon bits to sprinkle on the cheese.

Ice-cold milk from the Kingsleys' guernsey cow was passed around. I poured some for myself, then waited until everyone else had started eating before I picked up my fork.

James and Jones were fighting.

"Mom," Jones whined, "James stole my broccoli!"

"It wasn't yours. It was mine," James said, popping a piece into his mouth. "Besides, I was at the table before you were."

"You were not. I was here before you. I just had to go to the bathroom."

"That's your problem."

"Boys, boys! Settle down and eat." Mrs. Kingsley raised her voice above their bickering.

"What did you learn today?" Mr. Kingsley asked as soon as the boys were quiet. Mr. Kingsley insisted that everyone learn something every day. They could look up a word in the dictionary or measure a wall, but they had to learn something.

"I learned that Seychelles is the smallest country in Africa," Jones said with a grin. "It's a tiny group of islands in the Indian Ocean east of Tanzania."

It didn't take me long to figure out that

Jones looked in the encyclopedia or the almanac each night before dinner to memorize his tidbit for the day.

"I learned long division today, and I got 100 percent on my math test," James said.

James had been confined to a wheelchair because he'd had fluid on his spine when he was a baby. But whatever he lacked in body movement, he made up for with mind movement. He was the smartest fifth grader I'd ever known. In fact, he was smarter than a lot of teenagers I had known.

"That's excellent, James," replied Mr. Kingsley—Pop, as I was beginning to call him.

"How about you, Francis?" Mom asked.

"I learned that they need a part-time braille transcriber at Sheldon library, and I'm planning to apply for the job," Francis said.

"Isn't that where Saul Blackwell works?" Jones teased.

"That's enough, Jones. No one interrupted you. That's a great idea, Francis," Pop said.

"I want to use the money I earn to buy a new spellcheck software package for my talking computer," she added. "Then I'll have my own personal proofreader."

"I think I can get you a discount at work, hon," Pop said. "I met a woman from a place called Tri Visual Services the other day. She mentioned that they had some kind of lending library of speech software. For the cost of a disk, you can get a copy of anything they have."

"Good, then I'll use the money to buy disks," Francis said.

"The lady said that they have workshops every month to demonstrate new products."

"I want more time on the computer," James said. "I have the program for a new talking game, but it's going to take me a couple of hours to input it."

"You can use the computer tonight," Francis offered. "I'm done with my homework."

"I want to play, too," Jones chimed in.

"We'll see," Pop said. "Now let's get back to what we learned."

No matter what anyone said, the whole group seemed to be excited for that person. I wondered what I should say I learned today.

My turn came sooner than I'd expected. "Well, Janet," Pop said. "Did you enjoy your first day at school?"

I swallowed my bite of potato and looked at the friendly faces around the table. "I learned that I'm going to be in a play," I blurted out. "I'm going to paint scenery, too." I don't know why I said that. Being in a play wasn't really something I learned. It was just something I was going to do. I stared at my plate for a second, trying to think of something better to say. I wished I'd looked up something like Jones had.

"That's terrific, Janet!" Rosemary exclaimed. "You didn't tell me you were an actress."

"It's just a small part, but I'm really excited about it," I said. The family enthusiasm seemed to be catching.

"Do we get to go?" James asked, twirling around in his wheelchair.

"Park it, James!" Pop scowled.

"Of course we do," Francis chimed in. "We have to be Janet's fan club."

I blushed at their suggestion. "It's just a little part," I reminded them. "You'll probably be disappointed."

Mom put her hand on mine. "You'll soon learn, Janet, that nothing is too small or too unimportant in this family."

I looked around the table as everyone began eating again and the "What we learned today" conversation continued. I watched Jones cut his potato with the knife in his hook. He didn't complain if it took him longer to eat than the rest of us. He did it himself. Francis couldn't even see what was on her plate. But she served herself and poured her juice as well as any of us with just the help of her little finger over the rim of the glass. Biff missed most of the table conversation if he wasn't careful. It took him longer than the rest to eat, because he was always busy watching everyone's lips.

I still didn't know why the county had placed me in this home, but I was beginning to be glad they had. It was nice to be liked just for me, not for the things I could do or the money sent by foster care.

After dinner, I started to help Biff with the dishes, my chore for this week. For some reason, Trish's words kept ringing in my head. *Regs and crips don't mix,* she'd explained while we were getting dressed after P.E. *I know you rode the bus with them, but that doesn't mean you have to be friends with them. Everyone feels sorry for them. So do I,* she'd added with a sour expression. *But I don't have to get near them.*

Why I hadn't explained to Trish right then about my home situation, I don't know. I was afraid she wouldn't want to be my friend if she knew where I lived.

"Are you on another planet?" Biff waved his hand in front of my face.

"Oh, sorry," I said, turning toward him. "No, I was just thinking."

"About handicaps?" he asked perceptively. Then he continued before I could answer. "I hear you met David Williams in drama today."

"How did you hear that?" I looked at him suspiciously.

"David told me," he said simply as he handed me a plate. "He likes you."

"I only said a few words to him." I shook my head. "How does he know he likes me?" I couldn't help being pleased. When I'd talked to David this afternoon, he'd seemed like someone I'd like to know better.

"So you like him, too," Biff said. He was watching my eyes.

"How can you tell?" I asked as I finished loading the plastic glasses onto the rack in the dishwasher.

"Look at me, Janet. I can't see your lips when you have your head down."

"You see too much." I slapped him playfully with a sponge.

"It's just that your eyes talk even when your mouth doesn't," Biff said. "It's a trick I have for knowing what people are really saying. It's the same thing you do when you listen to the tone of people's voices or watch what they do with their bodies."

"Okay, so David seems nice," I admitted. "But he had to write his name down on paper for me. Why can't he talk like you can?"

"I lost my hearing when I was nine years old. There was a loud explosion near me that blasted out my eardrums," Biff explained. "I already knew how to talk, so I learned how to read lips and just kept talking. I know sign language, too. It comes in handy for watching television or listening to a speech when the person talking is too far away to see."

I scraped the leftovers into plastic bowls and waited.

"David has been almost completely deaf since birth," Biff went on. "His hearing aids help him hear loud sounds and some voices, but mainly he signs and writes."

"Why can't he talk if he can hear some sounds?"

Biff was quiet for a minute. "I think he can, but he just doesn't want to. He's embarrassed about what people will think of his voice. It's easier for him to be the shy-artist-type. Then everyone leaves him alone."

I dried the pans while I thought about David. He was super-talented and very nice. I really wanted to be able to talk to him while we paint scenery.

"Will you teach me some signs, Biff? I'm going to be doing props and scenery with David, and well, you know . . ."

Biff grinned and threw up both hands with his palms facing forward. Then he made a fist and shook his hand up and down.

"Okay," I said, laughing. "What does that mean?"

"It means 'Wonderful, I'll do it'!"

"How do you say, 'Thanks'?"

Biff put his fingers to his lips then let his hand fall forward like he was blowing me a kiss.

I threw my hands up and then blew him a kiss. "Wonderful," I said. "Thank you."

Six

THE next day I walked to school. When the Kingsley kids asked why, I just shrugged and told them I needed the exercise. Rosemary had given me a funny look. But she hadn't said anything. Biff offered to walk with me, but I turned him down. I gave him some excuse about needing to be alone to get my thoughts ready for the day.

After three weeks of walking to and from school, no one bothered to ask me anymore why I did it. I even had myself convinced that the brisk early morning walks and leisurely late afternoon strolls were good for me.

I had lots of time to think, and there was a lot to think about. School was great! Trish and Bridget were good friends. We did everything together, except go over to each other's houses.

Every day I met new people, all in the most

popular crowd at school. People liked me. *Would they though,* I wondered, *if they knew where I live and who I live with?* I wasn't going to chance having them find out. I avoided the Kingsleys at lunch and tried to pretend I didn't see them if we passed in the halls. I knew I was being mean, but I tried to make up for it by being extra nice at home.

Then there was the play and David. He was a really neat guy. All day long I waited for drama class so I could spend time with him. I'd show him the new signs Biff had taught me. Then David would show me some more, and I practiced them at home on Biff.

One day I waltzed into drama class in a great mood. I'd learned the signs for *surprise* and *obey.* Now I could say "I'm surprised you did or didn't obey." I wasn't sure what good it would do me, but it was fun anyway.

"Hey, hey, hey, Janet, baby!" Rad came up to me doing his Yogi Bear imitation. "Ready to practice your lines?"

My heart skipped a beat as it always did when Rad said anything to me. He was the most popular guy in our class, and I was never sure why he wanted to talk to me.

I just smiled and hoped he wouldn't notice how nervous I was. "I only have two lines," I joked. "If I don't know them by now, we have a big problem." I noticed that as I said "big," I made the *big* sign with my fingers in front of me.

Rad noticed, too. He frowned. "You've been hanging out with that dumbbell backstage too long. Oh, never mind. Have you studied someone else's part so we can prove how versatile we are to Herr Schmidt today?"

I put my hands down and willed them to remain motionless by my side while I talked. "I looked at a few lines."

"Which part did you study?" he asked.

"The lead. Who else?" I said, letting him take it in. "Mr. Schmidt assigned it to me," I added.

Rad smiled one of his I-know-everyone's-crazy-about-me smiles. "Then I guess you'll be working with me."

"I guess so." I turned and dropped gracefully into my seat as befit my character. I was going to play a princess for the day. I hoped Rad hadn't noticed that my knees were shaking.

Luckily when it came time to run through our parts, Mr. Schmidt had us do the beginning of the second act where the princess is in the woods. So I did a scene with Barry Marks instead of Rad. I threw myself into the role. I faked a stumble over a fallen log in the imaginary forest. I really had the class and Barry convinced that I'd actually hurt myself.

Slowly, I hobbled to a stool that was covered with brown material. It was supposed to be a stump, and I eased myself down on it. "Oh, pray, kind sir," I begged of the woodsman. "Do not leave me here in these dark woods alone. Night nears, and I have need of a cozy cottage in which to rest my weary head."

The class giggled as I batted my eyelashes and gazed pleadingly up into Barry's face. It was all he could do to remember his lines. I noticed David watching me from behind the curtain, and I made my actions even more expressive for his benefit.

When the scene was over, the whole class clapped for us. Barry shook my hand and said, "Anytime you need a leading man, just call me."

"I'll remember that," I said. It felt good to receive praise from Barry and my class. "Well, we were the last act, so I'd better get back to my props. I noticed that the stump wasn't very sturdy."

I slipped backstage and found David sitting in his usual place. He was painting lines between the bricks on a chimney. The windows to the multipurpose room were open, but the smell of latex paint still hung in the air around the stage. I walked over to David.

I took the curtains Mom had helped me sew out of my bag and slid them onto the wooden dowels we used for curtain rods.

"What do you think?" I signed to David as soon as I'd hung the rod in place above the open window on the finished cottage.

"Looks like home," he signed back. "Too bad you not princess to look out window. You make good princess." He blushed as his hands told me the words.

I didn't always know everything he was saying, but I was getting better at piecing his signs together. I wished I knew more. All I knew how to sign back for his compliment about my performance was *thank-you.* There were so many words I still had to figure out.

I started working on the stump. Just as I'd thought, one of the legs on the stool was loose. David handed me the glue, and I fixed it.

"What's next?" I asked him.

He placed my hands on the wooden cutout cottage. "Hold this," he instructed.

I steadied the second house while David moved some junk away from the wall. Then we propped the painted flat against the wall to finish drying.

David motioned for me to wait where I was. He went over to his sketch pad and ripped off the top sheet. Without another sign, he brought the sheet back and handed it to me. It was a drawing of me, but I hardly recognized myself. The face looked like me. But the hair was lots longer than mine. And he had it flowing around me and curling into the cloud I was riding on.

"No one has ever drawn a picture of me before." I stumbled on my words. "It's really pretty. Thank you." I blushed.

He blushed back.

"Have you done art long?" I asked him, signing the words I knew, *art* and *long*.

"Since little boy," he signed. He rubbed his thumbs and fingers together to ask me something. I only recognized the word *long* at the end. I shook my head, not understanding.

He took out his pad and wrote, "Glued stools long?"

I laughed. "Since little girl," I signed back.

Class was almost over. We didn't want to start a new project that couldn't be finished, so we just sat and talked. Well, signed and wrote, actually.

David told me he was an only child. "I envy the Kingsleys' big family. You must be happy there," he wrote.

I was kind of shocked that he knew where I lived. He hadn't said anything before. But of course he and Biff were friends, so I guessed Biff must have told him.

"Are you sorry I know?" he wrote. A frown of concern creased his forehead. "Biff said you walk to school and that none of the other kids know you live with them."

So Biff knew why I didn't ride the bus. That meant I probably hadn't fooled the rest of the family either. Now I felt twice as bad.

"No," I told him honestly. I was glad he could read lips, because I was way beyond my lessons here. "I'm not sorry you know." I touched his hand. "I really don't know why I haven't mentioned it earlier. All the other kids . . . they're so . . ."

He touched his index finger on his forehead and snapped the fingers of his right hand into his left palm. I didn't understand the hand signal, and David had to finger-spell it for me.

"Yes, prejudiced," I repeated, mimicking the sign he'd shown me.

We sat for a few minutes in silence.

David tapped my arm and pointed to his pad.

"What do you like to do besides paint and act?" I read. His smile told me he wanted to lighten the mood.

"I like to swim and skate and read," I told him. "How about you?" I pointed to his chest.

"I like to fly radio controlled airplanes," he wrote. Then he signed the words afterward to teach me.

He shook his fist up and down for yes when I asked if he built them himself. Of course, I knew the answer before I asked. He was so good at little tiny details.

"Want to go flying with me this Saturday?" He hesitated a little as he wrote it on the paper.

"I'd love to," I said. At the same time I shook my fist up and down.

We settled on a time just as the bell with the flashing light above it rang, dismissing school. David took off to catch his bus, but I took my time. It was my way of missing the bus without being obvious about it.

Trish and Bridget walked with me out of the parking lot. "Hey, how come you disappeared today? Everyone wanted to congratulate you on your performance. You were really super."

"Yeah," Bridget agreed. "You know the class likes you when they keep their mouths shut while you're up on the stage."

I remembered the performance and felt good again. I thought about telling Trish and Bridget that I was going to spend Saturday at the flying field with David Williams.

I watched as they made faces at the last

handicapped bus as it left the lot. No, telling them about David would take too much explaining. I checked to make sure his drawing of me was safely tucked inside my binder. I decided not to mention the picture either. I just hummed as I watched them cross the street at the light, and I turned to make my way toward home.

Seven

"SOMEBODY'S singing a happy tune," Rad said, magically appearing by my side.

I looked up, startled to see him.

"You should be happy," he continued. "Not only did you do a great job in class today, Princess Janet, but you get to go out with me this weekend."

Did he say what I thought he said? Rad Russell, Mr. Popularity, was asking me out? I couldn't believe it. He had so many girlfriends he practically had to peel them off like banana skins.

"What?" He laughed. "Nothing to say?"

Wait until Trish and Bridget hear about this, I thought. They'd both gone places with Rad and thought he was the greatest. Maybe he was just kidding me.

"Did you just ask me to go somewhere with

you?" I stammered, blushing furiously.

"There'll be a bunch of us, actually. I'm going to be in a skateboarding competition this weekend out at the Sheldon Sports Complex. Of course I'll win," he said with total confidence. "But I'd like you to be there to cheer me on."

"I'll have to ask my parents, but it sounds like fun," I told him. "Who else is going?"

"Barry, Rick, Bridget and Trish," he told me. "But they've all seen me ride. You're in for the thrill of your life. I'll even do a new stunt just for you, okay?"

"Okay," I said, feeling excited about all the attention. *First David and now Rad. David, oh no! I'd said I'd go to the flying field with him on Saturday.* I crossed my fingers and asked Rad when the competition was.

"Saturday at noon," he said.

I groaned. "I was afraid of that. I can't go." I watched his face as I broke the news to him. "I have something else planned."

His face fell. He looked like a lamb heading for the shearing shed. "Can't go?" he whined. "I'm crushed!" He placed his hands over his heart and staggered as if in pain. "I'm wounded. I may as well end it all right here!"

He whirled around, jerked twice, and sprawled on the grass alongside the road.

"Get up, Rad. People are staring at us."

He didn't move.

"Come on, Rad. I can't help it if I'm busy. I wish I wasn't, but I can't cancel now."

He still lay there not moving, but said in a half whisper, "I'll get up only if you say you'll go. Otherwise I'll lie right here all night long. I'll probably be dead before morning. They're expecting a heavy frost, you know."

"Hey, miss!" a man driving by in a car shouted. "Is everything all right?"

I was so embarrassed. Every car slowed down to stare. "Yes," I said softly, feeling my stomach flip over and grind to a halt.

Rad opened his eyes. "Did you say yes?"

"Yes, I said yes," I remarked impatiently. "Now, do me a favor and get up."

He jumped up, completely recovered. "See you then." He grinned and bounded off in the direction of the bike racks.

I didn't bound. I trudged. What was I going to tell David?

* * * * *

"Rad Russell is bad news," Rosemary lashed out. "If you never set eyes on him again, it would be too soon."

Rosemary and I were sitting in the barn, and

she was showing me how to milk the cow—her cow. She told me how she raised it on a bottle as a calf. "Jessie thinks I'm her mother."

She laughed as I aimed for the bucket and the stream of warm milk hit me in the face instead.

"I'll never fill the bucket at this rate," I complained good-naturedly.

"Just keep trying. You'll get it."

We did pretty well if we sat next to each other and squeezed together—a team effort. The squirting milk filled the silver bucket, and I thought about what Rosemary had said earlier about Rad.

"What am I supposed to do, Rosemary? I told them both, David and Rad, I'd go someplace with them on the same day."

"I guess you have to decide who you want to be with most," she said, "a jerk who likes himself better than anyone else or a friend like David. It's your decision."

"But Rad may never ask me out again if I don't go this time. Trish and Bridget will think I'm crazy."

"You are if you let them run your life. They're not very good friends if you can't tell them the truth about who you are and where you live!"

"It's my business whether I tell them or

not," I told her. I was really kind of ashamed, but I let myself get angry to cover it. And I guess I took it out on poor Jessie.

"You'd better quit trying to milk her. You're scaring her," Rosemary said. She pushed my hand out of the way and patted Jessie's side.

I dried my hands on a towel and waited until Rosemary was finished. Then I helped her lift the heavy bucket onto the cart.

"The problem is not going to go away, you know." Rosemary released the cow's neck from the milking stand. Then she patted Jessie on the nose and fed her some fresh grass.

Rosemary turned to me. "Sooner or later," she said, "you'll have to tell people where you live. It was hard for me when I came here, too. The Trishes and Rads of this town don't make it any easier. You're setting yourself up for a big letdown if you don't face facts now. And poor David . . ."

"Where did you live before you came here?" I asked, wanting to change the subject. I didn't want to think about poor David or poor Rad or poor me.

Rosemary continued petting the cow while she gazed off into space. She shook her head. "At a children's hospital."

"You lived there all your life?" I asked in

amazement. "I thought you were a . . ." I stopped myself before I said reg.

She ignored my slip. "Well, not all my life. First I lived with my parents, but they beat me too many times, and the county took me away from them."

"Do you ever see them? Do you miss them?"

"I don't even remember them very well." Her voice broke as she told me about how she'd been abused. She said she ended up at a rehabilitation facility until she was seven. Then she finally came to live with the Kingsleys.

"At least you had a family that loved you, Janet," she told me softly. "I'm sorry they died," she added.

"It was really hard right after they died. It didn't seem like anyone cared. People just shoved me around from place to place. Even now, I don't know how long I'll get to stay here."

"I thought Mom and Pop were trying to adopt you."

"Other families have said that, but then they sent me back. The way I've been treating you guys, I wouldn't blame any of you if you didn't want me to stay."

"Everybody here knows that it takes time. We've all had to go through something. If you'd just try to look past the handicaps and see who we really are, I think you'd be surprised at how 'regular' this family is," she said.

"Do you ever wonder about your birth parents?" Rosemary asked. "The rest of us do. That's something we all have in common, you know."

She was right. I'd been so busy thinking about regs and crips that I hadn't thought about it. None of us lived with our birth parents.

I nodded my head. "Yeah, I started to think about mine after the Martins died. But why would you wonder about yours? They treated you so horribly."

Her eyes took on a faraway look again. But then she turned back to me and said, "I'd just like to show them what they missed by giving me up."

I went over and put my hand on her shoulder. I was beginning to feel very close to Rosemary. "They missed a lot," I said.

"This doesn't solve your problem with Rad and David, does it?" she asked as we rolled the milk cart up to the kitchen door.

"I guess I'm going to have to solve that one on my own."

"Don't wait too long, Janet."

Eight

BY Saturday I was a wreck. Bridget and Trish had already called four times each. They wanted to plan what to wear to the skateboard competition. And they talked about how much money to bring for snacks.

I sighed as I put down the phone for the eighth time that morning.

Ring. Ring. I picked up the receiver again expecting it to be Trish or Bridget. Instead it was Rad.

"Hey," he grunted. "Plans have changed. I have to be at the skateboard arena an hour early to warm up."

When I didn't say anything, he softened his voice. "You aren't fixing to back out on me are you, Jan? You did get out of those other plans you had, didn't you?"

This was the perfect opportunity to tell Rad that I hadn't been able to get out of my other commitments and would just have to cancel. But part of me kept thinking how great it would be to be seen by everyone as Rad's choice. And the words just wouldn't come.

"Well?" he demanded.

I cleared my throat. "No, everything's fine, Rad. I'll be there."

"Great," he said, like he knew all the time what my answer would be. "My parents are driving the rest of us. Are you sure we can't pick you up?"

"Positive," I repeated. "I'd rather meet you at the sports complex. I'll enjoy the walk."

I hung up the phone and turned to find Rosemary leaning against the kitchen door. "I'll bet you've never walked so much in your life," she remarked. "Have you told David yet?" she asked more sympathetically.

I shook my head. "Are you mad at me, Rosemary?"

"What's to be mad at? It's your life. I already gave you my opinion. You did what you thought you had to do," she replied. "I know you felt you had no choice."

I slumped down in the padded chair next to the phone table. "If I had no choice, why do I feel so bad?"

"Because you should."

She wasn't there when I looked up again. I

reached for Biff's computer phone for deaf people and dialed David's number. At least I didn't have to see his face or hear his disappointment when I typed my message over the TDD machine. It was almost like writing him a letter.

"Hello, this is David." The words ran across the read-out screen.

"This is Janet," I typed. "I'm sorry. I can't go flying with you today. Something else came up." It sounded dumb. But I didn't want to tell him the truth, and I didn't want to lie.

"That's okay, Janet." His words flew over the screen. "We'll go another time. Bye."

"Bye," I typed to the screen in David's house, knowing he had already hung up.

Was he upset? Who knew? Words across a printed screen couldn't tell you much. Biff was right, you have to see people's faces and look at their eyes to know how they're feeling.

I thought about David's eyes. They were clear and bluish green, like water with trees reflected in it. Sometimes when we were painting scenes together, I would catch myself just staring into David's eyes. Then he would smile and I would smile, and I wouldn't even feel stupid for looking at him that way. I felt like a rat for standing him up like this.

I found Mom and Pop and told them I was

leaving early. "I really love this shirt," I told her as I fingered the blue and green material that matched Jones' shirt. It reminded me of David's eyes, and I wished I was wearing it for him instead of Rad.

"Well, it looks great on you, Janet. I was glad to make it. I'm working on something else for you now," she hinted. "But I can't tell you about it just yet."

I smiled and hugged her. "You're really the nicest foster mother and father I've had," I told them. And then I hoped I wasn't being too pushy.

"We hope you'll soon consider us more than just temporary foster parents, Janet." Pop came over to get a hug, too.

"Don't put so much pressure on her, Bob," Mom said. She dropped a kiss on his beard, then turned to me. "Get going now, honey, and have a good day. There's plenty of time to make major decisions later."

The air was almost cold as I half walked, half trotted the two miles to the sports complex. I could still feel the wind's chilly fingers poking at me through the sweater Mom had made me take along just in case.

They really were the nicest foster family I'd stayed with in the last two years. But was I ready to be adopted by them? I knew that's what Pop was talking about when he said to think of them as more than temporary.

I hadn't even told my best friends at school where I lived. I walked every day to avoid their questions about why I had ridden on a handicapped bus. And I was walking two miles today to avoid telling Rad where I lived and having his parents pick me up.

I couldn't keep the truth hidden for much longer. Right now I was Janet Martin at school. What would happen when the time for the play came and the Kingsleys showed up for family night? I couldn't tell them not to come. All the kids were so excited about me being in the play.

What if I officially became Janet Kingsley? Would Trish and Bridget and Rad still want to be friends with me? They considered the Kingsleys retards and crips. And they would see me that way, too.

Regs and crips don't mix. The words echoed in my brain. I knew down deep that the Kingsleys weren't retarded or contagious in any way. Trish and Bridget and Rad were wrong in the way they thought. But still, I didn't want to mess up my only chance at popularity. If there was only some way to have both.

I knew by now that Mr. and Mrs. Kingsley probably wouldn't turn me away like the other foster homes had. Mrs. Shelley was right when she said the Kingsleys didn't send kids back no matter what. Their family was made up of "no matter what's."

I knew that if I wanted to stay there permanently, I could. The choice would be mine, because of my age. The judge would ask me if I liked the Kingsleys and wanted to be adopted. Sweat beads broke out across my forehead even though the day was chilly. What a mess.

The Sheldon Sports Complex was just ahead. It was huge. A large building labeled Youth Center stood in the middle shaded by huge oak and walnut trees. On the left were baseball diamonds, a football and soccer field, several basketball courts, and even an outdoor skating rink. Kids were everywhere.

"Hi, Janet," someone called. I raised my hand to wave and was greeted by more kids. The indecision I'd felt earlier turned to a warm glow. It felt great to be popular.

I saw the banked cement curves of the skateboard arena. Beyond that was an open field.

There was quite a crowd already waiting to watch the skateboard event. Trish yelled and waved as soon as I entered the gate. I made my way up the steps between the benches and sat beside her and Barry. Bridget and Rick were off hitting baseballs or something, she told me.

"Where's Rad?"

Barry pointed to a rider in a gold helmet with matching gloves, knee pads, and elbow protectors. Rad was poised at the top of a steep ramp. He lifted his wheels and plunged down. His speed took him up the ramp on the other side where he hugged into the curve, spun around, and sped down again.

"Wow!" My breath caught in my throat.

"I told you he was good," Trish gushed. I wondered what Barry thought about her drooling over Rad. He probably hadn't noticed. He had the same thrilled expression on his face, too.

It was true. Rad was good. No one else I saw out there warming up was even close to him in speed and style. I caught the excitement as I watched the practice rides.

"I'm going to get something to drink before they start. Want anything?" I asked Trish and Barry, and Bridget and Rick who had just joined us.

They gave me their orders, and I went to stand in the refreshment line.

I saw Francis in line and said hello. She introduced me to the guy she was with. It was

Saul Blackwell. I smiled as I said hi to him, though he couldn't see me. Saul was blind, too. He was taller than Francis, and they looked good together. I wished Francis could see how cute he was. I guessed that appearances didn't matter much to them, though.

"Oh, by the way, Janet, I found the earring you lost in our room last night," Francis said. She laughed, knowing I'd probably wonder how she found something so tiny. "I knelt down to get my shoes out from under the bed, and it poked me in the knee. I put it on your dresser."

"Thanks," I told her as she turned to Saul to explain that I'd only been living at her house for a few weeks, but that I made a good roommate.

"Is anyone else from the family here?" I asked cautiously, wondering if today was the day I was going to be found out.

"Just Biff," she told me. "He's over there." Francis pointed to the field I'd seen behind the arena. "The last time I checked, he and David Williams were getting ready to fly their planes. See you later."

"It was nice meeting you, Janet," Saul said.

"You, too," I echoed.

As Francis and Saul walked away, a sinking feeling hit me.

The flying field. Why hadn't I thought of it before? Of course the flying field would be part of the sports complex.

Just as I turned to look for David and Biff, they looked up and saw me, too. I watched in horror as they started toward me. David had that special grin stuck all over his face. He thought I'd come to go flying with him after all. Biff had a funny expression, like something bad was going to happen.

"Hey, Janet!" I heard a voice boom behind me. "Did you see me ride? What style! What grace! What tight maneuvers! Janet?"

I didn't answer. All I could do was look back and forth between Rad and David. David's smile was rapidly turning into a frown.

Then Rad did a really stupid thing. He put his arm around me. I tried to shrug it off. But he held it there and stuck his face right in my face.

He stuck his tongue out and panted a few times. "What's a guy got to do to get a little attention around here?" Rad asked, looking like a sad little puppy dog.

I couldn't help but laugh. "Sorry, Rad. I was a million miles away," I said.

"Just a couple hundred feet, I'd say." He glanced in the direction I'd been looking. David and Biff were walking away now.

"What do you mean?" I forced myself to look at Rad and not to watch to see if David turned around again. David's eyes had told it all. Even from a distance, I knew he knew I'd stood him up to go out with Rad.

Rad waved his hand in David and Biff's direction. "Those hand wigglers aren't worth worrying about. You're better off with me," he stated simply.

What a selfish, inconsiderate attitude. Who did he think he was anyway? I was about to tell him off when I suddenly reached the front of the line and had to give the cashier my order. When I turned around to yell at him, he was gone.

I got the drinks and headed back to the bleachers. As I slipped onto the bench beside Bridget, a voice on the loudspeaker was announcing the first skateboard event.

"What happened over there?" Bridget asked. "I saw that dumb David guy you do props with heading your direction."

"He's not dumb!" I said.

"Oh, come on, Janet," Trish said, frowning. "Everyone knows he can't hear and he can't talk."

"He can so talk. He talks with his hands in sign language," I told them.

"Just because you have to work props with

him in drama class doesn't mean you have to be friends with him," Bridget said.

"We saw you talking to those blind kids, too," Trish accused.

"I was only being polite," I said.

"Oh, come on, Janet. They wouldn't even know you were there if you didn't talk first," Trish went on.

Now was as good a time as any to break the news. "Well, I had to say something. Francis is . . ."

"Forget about dumb David Williams and those other crips. Watch the show," Trish interrupted. "Oooh, look," she squealed. "I'll bet Rad's going to win the trophy again!"

Nine

I tried to forget about David while I watched Rad spin and twirl and speed along on his four-wheeled "Sandblaster," as he called it. I kept looking over my shoulder to see if Biff and David were still in the flying field.

Finally I saw them packing up to leave. I turned back to the skateboard competition with a sigh of relief. Now that I didn't have to worry about running into them again, I could concentrate on Rad.

"You're really lucky Rad asked you to come today, you know, Janet," Trish whispered in my ear. "Every girl in school wishes he'd ask her to cheer for him."

I knew I'd better get my act together or I'd never be asked along again. I took a deep breath.

"Hey, look at that spin!" I shouted. "All right, Rad! Go for it!"

"That's more like it," Trish said with a grin. "If you keep that up, he'll ask you out again."

"What makes you think so?" I asked, trying to keep my concentration on the arena.

"He told me," she said simply. "He's fascinated by your mysterious side."

I couldn't help but feel a little flattered by her statement. After all, Rad *was* the most popular guy in the whole junior high.

For the next half hour we yelled our encouragement and oohed and aahed Rad's daring feats. Finally we gave a rousing cheer as Rad emerged victorious with a blue ribbon and a trophy.

"I told you I'd win," he said, coming up to me. His eyes were shining after the ceremony.

I pushed David firmly to the back of my mind and gave Rad my best smile. "I never doubted it for a minute," I told him.

He threw his arm around my shoulder again, and I forced myself not to push it away. Trish was looking at us like she'd created a fairytale. Bridget just stood with her mouth open like she couldn't believe my luck.

* * * * *

I dreaded going to drama class the next Monday. I dawdled in the room, pretending to study my two lines and rehearse my part. Finally Mr. Schmidt handed me a box of props and sent me backstage.

David was sorting dishes, lamps, and books into boxes marked Scene 1, Scene 2, and Scene 3.

What was I going to say to him? Last night I'd looked up the sign for "I'm sorry" in the dactylology book. But somehow it didn't seem like enough.

I might as well get it over with, I told myself. I walked over to where David stood with his back to me. I put my box down on the table beside his three boxes and started sorting like he was.

Our hands touched over the Scene 2 box. He looked up, and I looked up. I raised my hands to speak, but he pushed them down. He stared at me for a long time.

"Pass me the books," he finally signed.

I handed him the books, and we spent the next 15 minutes filling boxes in silence.

Even though we weren't talking, I felt more comfortable sitting backstage with David than I ever felt with Rad.

In the middle of my thoughts, I heard my name and David's being called out front.

"I would like the whole class to hear this announcement," Mr. Schmidt said. One of the kids in the back of the room signed to translate for the deaf kids.

"Sherry Whitcomb was to play Princess Matilda, the lead for our play. But you may have noticed that Sherry isn't here today."

We looked around wondering what he would say next.

"I've just received word from on high, the office," he clarified, "that Miss Whitcomb has had a family emergency and will be attending school in Arizona for the rest of the term."

The class gasped in unison.

"Therefore," Mr. Schmidt pronounced, "I am turning over the leading role to . . ." Someone tapped out a drumroll on a desktop. "Janet Martin!"

"Three cheers for my new leading lady," Rad said, raising his arm in the air.

When the hoorays died down, I was still trying to catch my breath. I was going to play the part of Matilda. I'd be doing 10 scenes with Rad. We'd have to practice together a lot so I could catch up on Sherry's part.

"But what about props?" I asked as I watched David slowly turn and disappear behind the curtain. His face was unreadable, and his hands were still.

"We'll get someone else to help David," Mr. Schmidt replied. He waved at the boy who had been translating his speech into signs and asked him to go backstage.

"Better get to work, Matilda." Rad put his arm around me again. "Here's your new script. Come on, I'll read lines with you."

As the days slipped by I saw less and less of David and more and more of Rad. The whole school thought of us as a couple. Bridget and Trish were thrilled. I didn't know what to think.

Despite all my other problems I was really having fun rehearsing for my new role as Matilda. The play was only a few weeks away. Every night I'd read my lines to Rosemary. I practiced until I'd memorized a whole scene. Then the next day I'd practice the full scene with Rad.

Mr. Schmidt was very impressed with how fast I learned my part. So was Rad.

The Kingsleys looked forward to my upcoming performance with as much excitement as I did. One night, James and Jones paraded around the living room reciting passages from my scenes. You'd have thought they were going to be the actors instead of Rad and me.

At school the next day we were putting the finishing touches on the final scene. I wasn't really into the part. I was thinking about James wheeling around playing Marcus and Jones leaning on his cane playing Matilda the night before. I realized that I still hadn't told the kids at school where I was living. And I still hadn't apologized to David for the day at the sports complex.

"You're not with me, Janet," Rad hissed. "I've given you your cue three times."

I dragged my thoughts back to the drama room and tried to remember where I'd left off in the scene. I frowned.

"I'm so glad you've come back to me, Marcus . . ." Rad whispered my line to me.

I stared out the imaginary window a moment longer. I tried to pull myself back into the character of a furious sister about to give her long-lost brother a piece of her mind.

I turned to face Rad. "I'm so glad you've come back to me, Marcus," I sneered, making an angry grimace. "I've been waiting so long to give you this gift . . ."

"A gift for me?" he said with just the right amount of innocence. "What is it, sister dear?"

"A conk on that fool head of yours!" I shouted.

With that, I ran toward him swinging a frying pan and hopping over furniture. I was aiming the pan at his head.

"No, Matilda, no!" he cried out in fear. "I didn't mean to gamble away your money." He vaulted over the couch and skidded across the rug. He'd been perfecting that move for weeks. "Please don't harm me! I didn't mean to shoot a hole in the castle roof trying to kill a fly. I didn't mean to sell your ball dresses for a . . ."

I chased him around and around the stage and then off into the wings. There I banged the metal pan onto an anvil that David had just set in place. The clanging sound echoed through the room as the curtain went down.

"Good! Good!" Mr. Schmidt clapped a few times. "Now let's do it again. And Janet, stay with the program, okay?"

"Okay." I smiled sheepishly. I went back to my place by the window, waiting for Rad to enter. David emerged from backstage to hand me my frying pan just before the curtain went up.

"Thanks," I signed, but he had already turned away. I wanted so badly to talk to him, but I never seemed to find the time. I always ate lunch with the drama gang and spent all my time in class working on my new part.

The lights dimmed. I tore my thoughts away from David and concentrated on the play.

The curtain went up. I stood motionless before the window, waiting for the lights to come on. The door slammed behind me.

I turned. "I'm so glad you've come back to me, Marcus . . ."

Ten

"NO. Move your hand like this. See?" Biff instructed me. "If you want to say that you're ashamed of yourself, you have to place the back of your curved hand against your cheek. Turn your hand over like you're covering your mouth."

"I am ashamed of myself," I said as I signed.

"Well, I'm tired of hearing about it." Biff went back to laying straw on the floor of the chicken coop. "You did what you thought you had to. I don't think you were right, but maybe David will understand."

I untied the wires on another bale of straw and chunked off a square section for Biff. "Did he tell you that he understood?" I asked.

"I don't think I should tell you what he said. I think you should go ask him yourself. None of the rest of us get our jobs done for us. We've all had to learn to stand on our own two feet, or whatever we have to stand on."

I sighed. It was another well-deserved lecture.

"You know, Janet, you're a mess. One minute you act like you want to live here, and the next minute you act like you hate us. You can't really have it both ways."

"Rosemary told me the same thing," I said. "I'm working on it."

We continued spreading straw until the floor was covered and sweet-smelling again. I picked up the wire egg basket and gathered eggs from the nests. Luckily, none of the chickens was there. They all flew out when Biff and I came in to clean.

"What are you so scared of?" He wouldn't let up. "Are you afraid you'll get a handicap by living with us? Or are you just afraid of getting a label like *retard* or *hand-wiggler* or *crip*?" He emphasized the word *crip* like it was the worst swearword in the English language.

"No, it's not that . . . " I began, but didn't know what else to say. Part of what he said was true.

"No, not that. Never that," he copied. "We're not stupid, Janet. The whole family knows why you walk to school and why you avoid us in the halls. You must think that handicapped people have no feelings. Don't you think we notice all the things you do to snub us?"

"It's just . . . it's just . . . that . . ." I started crying. I couldn't help it. All the fears and frustrations and worries of the past two years came to the surface in one big rush.

I sat down on the straw and buried my face in my hands. I wished with all my heart that when I opened my eyes I would be back home in my canopy bed and that my mother and father would be smiling down at me saying, *You're just having a bad dream, sweetie. We love you. It's time to wake up now.*

Biff sat down next to me and put his arm around my shoulders. "It's just that you want to be popular." I heard Biff's voice through my sobs and nodded my head. I looked up at him.

"You don't understand, Biff. For the past two years I've been an outcast wherever I went. No one cared that I'd lost my parents or that I'd left a lot of friends behind where I used to live. I was always the new girl, and no one ever tried to get to know me or include me until I came here. Then I met Trish and Bridget and Rad. And suddenly everyone likes me. I'm no longer Janet the foster child. I'm somebody special."

I sniffed. "I suppose that sounds selfish,

doesn't it?" I said through my tears.

Biff sat down next to me. "No, it sounds lonely. But don't you see? Every one of us has gone through something similar. We've all felt that no one cares. But when you came here, you did the same thing to us that people have been doing to you. You ignored us and didn't bother to get to know us. David, too. He's a really nice guy." Biff smiled. "You should at least take the time to talk with him and find that out. Then if you decide you like Rad Russell better, at least you know you gave them both a chance."

"When do I have time to talk to him? I only see him in class, and then I'm too busy."

"You aren't too busy today. I happen to know David is at the flying field this morning. He's going to try out a new Cessna twin-engine he just built."

"What about my chores?"

"I'll do them, and you can do mine tomorrow. Tell Mom we switched."

"Thanks, Biff," I told him, "for everything."

"It's okay to cry once in while, you know," Biff said.

I gave him a quick hug.

"Get out of here." Biff motioned me away.

I ran to ask Mom's permission.

* * * * *

I didn't want to walk to the sports complex, so I borrowed Biff's bike. He was really helping me out, just like I imagined a real brother would.

Mom and Pop had said that they wanted to talk to me about something important when I got home. And they said that Mrs. Shelley was coming over for dinner. In the back of my mind I had a pretty good idea about what they were going to bring up.

I put off thinking about the Kingsleys as I turned the corner into the sports complex and saw David in the flying field.

His blond hair shone in the golden sun. The silver airplane he carried flashed beams of light as the sun glinted off its surface.

I parked Biff's bike behind David and locked it to a post. For a minute I hesitated as I watched him set the remote controls and clear the small runway of debris.

I thought about all the hours Biff and the rest of the kids had spent teaching me sign language. I didn't know everything, but I knew enough to talk to David and say what I had to say.

Just like when we worked together backstage, I made my presence known by walking up beside him. I stood quietly while he revved the engines and taxied the homemade craft down the tiny runway.

My heart leaped into the air with the little plane as it quickly took off and gained altitude. David circled it around the airfield and brought it down in a perfect landing. Then he turned to me. There was a frown on his lips and a question in his eyes.

Suddenly all the words I had meant to sign floated away. I couldn't remember anything. The longer I looked into his beautiful, expressive eyes, the more I felt like crying again.

First one tear and then another rolled down my cheek. David reached up and brushed them away.

Why was he being so nice to me when I'd been so rotten to him?

I finally got a hold of myself. I faced him so he could read from my lips what I couldn't sign. "I'm so sorry, David. I didn't mean to hurt you. I'm sorry I cancelled our date to go out with Rad. I just . . . I just . . ."

"You didn't feel you had a choice?" he signed.

I nodded.

"There is always choice," he said in a raspy, flat-sounding voice. I couldn't believe that he'd spoken out loud. I was watching his hands. They said the same thing.

My tears stopped instantly.

"You can talk!" I said in surprise. "Why didn't you tell me before?"

"Your friends make fun of me. They think I'm stupid as well as deaf. It's easier to let them believe what they want to believe."

"But, David, I don't think you're stupid. Why didn't you tell me?"

"I thought you might be different. You tried to learn my language. But you were always with Rad." He spelled Rad's name. "I wasn't sure if you really liked me or you were just being nice to the deaf guy."

His words were bitter and hard to understand. He talked so fast, and the sounds ran together. But I knew what he was saying. He hadn't been sure he could trust me. I was friends with the regs and hadn't told anyone who I really was or where I lived.

"I was afraid to tell anyone where I lived," I admitted. "I was afraid they wouldn't want to be friends with me anymore. Now I don't care what they think. It doesn't matter anymore. I'd rather have real friends." The words sounded convincing enough. I hoped I was strong enough to carry through with what I was saying.

I laid my hand on David's arm as he carefully maneuvered the plane to the end of the tiny runway.

"Are you sure? Because when you come over to this side of the line, there's no going back." He turned to face me.

"You mean I can never be friends with a reg again?" I asked.

"No, it's not that bad. You'll find that there are quite a few kids who have both kinds of friends. But Trish and her gang won't accept you into their group."

I recalled my words to Rosemary. "Then they're missing a lot. I like you," I told him seriously. "I'd like you even if you weren't deaf." I know that sounded weird.

David's silent laughter broke the somber mood. "Even if I were hearing, you would?"

"I mean it wouldn't make any difference." He was laughing so hard I started laughing, too. It felt good.

"I know what you mean, Janet. I like you, too. I'd like you even if you were deaf."

When we finally stopped laughing, David handed me the controls to his plane. "Want to try?" he asked.

"Sure." I nodded my head and smiled. David smiled back and showed me how to work the controls. My takeoff was a little shaky, but I got the plane off the ground.

David came around in front of me as I tried to keep the plane in the air. "Don't jerk the stick. Go easy."

"The wing is tipping to the left. The plane wants to circle," I said anxiously.

"You're in control of the plane. You make it go. You have to take charge."

He was right. I had to take control . . . of more than just a little silver plane. We were talking about me and school and Rad and David and the Kingsleys. We were talking about my life, the one I needed to be in charge of.

"What about Rad?" he asked quietly.

I knew what he meant. The whole school thought we were going steady or something.

"The play is important to me," I said, speaking slowly so he could read my lips. I didn't want to chance taking my hands off the remote-control stick.

"Is Rad important to you?"

I risked taking one hand off the control long enough to draw a small heart on my chest to tell him how serious I was. "No," I said.

He touched his right hand to his lips and brought it down to rest in his open left palm. "Good."

Eleven

DAVID'S words echoed in my head all along the ride home. *Good,* he'd said when I told him that Rad wasn't important to me.

David had taught me a lot of things today besides how to fly his airplane. It didn't matter that his voice sounded like sandpaper. His feelings came through loud and clear. David wanted me to like him for himself, not because I felt sorry for him or because he could or couldn't hear.

A jet streaked overhead, and my heart soared along with it. I wasn't going to let my friends tell me what to think or do anymore. If I wanted to be friends with David, I would. Who cared what they thought? They would have to accept me the way I was. I chuckled to myself. I was beginning to think like a crip, and I liked it.

I sailed into the driveway, showering the split-rail fence with gravel. Mrs. Shelley's car was parked in front of the house.

"I'm glad you're home, Janet," she called from the garden where she was helping Mom lift two huge baskets of vegetables.

"Come on into the kitchen," Mom said. "Bob!" she called. "We're going to have that meeting now."

I was so happy after my talk with David that I had forgotten all about the meeting we were supposed to have. Were they going to say they wanted to adopt me? What if they said it wasn't working out? I thought everyone liked me here. But I'd been treating them pretty badly. My old fears about doing something awful came back in full force.

It seemed strange to be sitting around the big dining room table without the rest of the kids. In fact, the house seemed much too quiet as the four of us took our seats.

"How's everything going?" Mrs. Shelley asked politely.

"Everything's fine," I told her. "I like school. I'm going to be in a play . . ." I trailed off.

I chewed my nails. *Is something wrong?* I wondered again. *Are they going to send me to another foster home just when I'm finally fitting in?* I looked from Mrs. Kingsley to Mr. Kingsley and back to Mrs. Shelley.

"Don't look so worried, honey." Pop put his big rough hand over mine. "We like having you here. We know the kids at school have been giving you a hard time, but we've been letting you solve things on your own."

Even Mom and Pop know, I thought.

"In fact," Mom interrupted, "we're hoping you'll decide to stay."

My gaze took in their expectant faces. "I have a choice?" I asked. I knew I was supposed to, but I didn't believe it until now. "All the other homes sent me away. I didn't have a choice then."

Mrs. Shelley took a sip of the mint tea Mom placed in front of her. "The other homes didn't want to adopt you. The Kingsleys do," she explained. "But you do have a choice. Because of your age, you have the right to accept their offer. Or you can decide to continue in long-term foster care in another home until you're 18."

I felt myself beginning to relax as she spoke. They weren't going to send me away. They were asking me to be their daughter. I really had a choice. Suddenly I realized how much I wanted to stay. The Kingsleys had become my family more than any other I'd lived with in the past two years.

Still I had one more problem. "But I'm not handicapped like the others. Even Rosemary spent time in a children's hospital." It was more of a statement than a question.

"Honey, we're all handicapped in some way. I grew up an orphan," Mrs. Kingsley revealed. "It was terrible. I had no mother and father to love me or care for me, just the staff at the orphanage. Living that way was just as much of a handicap as the more obvious ones your brothers and sisters have. When Bob and I got married, we couldn't have our own children. So we decided to adopt a big family and give them all the love and caring they would have missed otherwise. And we have to warn you. There may be others."

More kids?

"We know the 'regs' at school can be difficult." It sounded funny hearing Pop using the term my friends used. "But, honey, they're the ones who are the most crippled," he went on. "Their prejudices keep them from being friends with a lot of nice kids."

Mrs. Shelley added, "You really have a very special role, Janet. You understand and like people on both sides. You could bring the two groups together."

I didn't know how good I'd be at closing the

big gap at school, but I knew one thing for sure. I wanted to become a Kingsley . . . forever.

The next week was a blur. I rode the bus to school every day, and I ate lunch with David, Biff, and Rosemary. I left quickly after drama every day, before Rad got the chance to ask any questions.

But on Friday, Rad caught up with me as I was climbing onto the bus. "I need to talk to you, Janet Martin," he insisted as he grabbed my arm. "What's gotten into you lately?"

"I really can't stay and talk. I have to be in court in an hour," I informed him without an explanation.

He was still standing on the sidewalk with his mouth open as we drove off.

By the time we arrived home I was a bundle of nerves. Would something go wrong at court? Would the judge decide I needed to live somewhere else? Would I be able to talk and not cry like a baby?

"Are you excited, Janet?" Rosemary and I were hurriedly getting dressed for the adoption hearing. The whole family was going, and then we were going to have a party at home afterward. Earlier today I had invited David to come to the party. Mom had told me to ask all of my friends from school, but David was the only person I wanted to invite.

"I can barely button my top," I told Rosemary. "My hands are shaking."

"It could be worse," Francis said as she struggled to fasten a complicated belt strap. "At least you can see what you're doing."

"I don't know about that. I've buttoned this up wrong twice now."

"I didn't notice," she joked.

"It's time to go," Biff called from the hall.

"They always send Biff so we can't argue back," Rosemary said.

We all giggled.

"Good thinking," I agreed. Life was pretty easy when you didn't take everything so seriously.

* * * * *

Finally we were in the judge's chambers in the courthouse. Mom and Pop and I sat in front of the judge's big desk. A lot of things were said, but I only remembered one thing during the whole hearing. That was when the judge asked Mr. and Mrs. Kingsley why they wanted to adopt me.

I held my breath.

"Because we love her," they both said at once.

Then the judge turned to me. "And do you want to belong to the Kingsley family?" he asked. His face was wrinkled, and his smile was warm. "Do you want to be adopted?"

For a long time I had waited for a judge to ask me that question.

I looked around at my brothers and sisters, and then I looked at Mom and Pop. "More than anything," I said. I let out the big breath that I'd been holding. "I love them, too."

We signed the papers and headed home. My new brothers and sisters were full of chatter, but I couldn't tear my eyes away from the rolling fields of golden grain, waving in the autumn heat. In the spring, the fields would be green again, and I'd be there to see them.

I wondered what my first mom and dad, the Martins, would think about where their little Janet was living? I was sure they'd be happy. They always wanted the best for me. But I still missed them. A part of me always would.

"Close your eyes," Francis instructed as we turned into our driveway.

"Why?" I asked, but I did it anyway.

"We have something to show you, and you can't peek until we're all in the house."

I did as they said and let them lead me inside.

"Okay, you can open your eyes," Francis

said, stopping me with a firm grasp.

I blinked.

"Surprise!" everyone shouted.

I couldn't believe it. The living room was hung with streamers and balloons. A big sign over the table spelled out "Welcome to the family, Janet Kingsley!" There was a huge lavender cake with lifelike darker purple flowers around the corners and edges. Right in the center of the cake was a shiny white ceramic kitten.

"It's so cute!" I said, running a finger along each smooth pink ear.

Pop left the room for a second and returned with his hands behind his back. "Every Kingsley has to have a mascot," he said. He brought his hands out from behind him. Curled in one big hand was a tiny Persian kitten, the twin for the one on the cake.

I cuddled the kitten to my cheek and thought about Rosemary's cow, Biff's chickens, Francis' puppy that was soon to be a guide dog, and the snakes that belonged to James and Jones. Mrs. Shelley had said the Kingsley children all had their own special pets. Now the newest Kingsley's pet was purring on my shoulder.

"Thank you," I said, noticing David for the first time standing behind the punch bowl.

Jones tugged me around the room showing me everything—the streamers, the tissue-paper flowers and chains, the cut-glass plates. He pointed to the sign. "I painted the letters," he said with pride.

"How did you manage to decorate?" I asked the group. "You were all with me at the courthouse."

"The room has been decorated most of the day," Rosemary said, laughing. "Mom just closed the parlor doors and you went upstairs after school without noticing."

"David set out all the finishing touches while we were gone," James said.

"Congratulations, Janet Kingsley," David said in his raspy voice.

I liked the sound of my new name. Tears glistened in my eyes as I held my kitten and looked at David and my new family.

"Looks like she needs a hug," Biff announced.

"HUGS!" James and Jones shouted and charged at me. For a few minutes I was lost in a big laughing-crying-pushing-shoving-hugging mass of Kingsleys. Somewhere in the middle, I know David hugged me, too. I felt warm all over and not scared anymore.

"This is turning out to be quite a week," David told me afterward as we sat eating cake and talking in voice and sign.

"I know. First we became friends again. Today I got adopted. And in a few days we'll do the play." I looked at him to see if my mentioning the play had hurt his feelings, but he was still smiling at me.

"You make a really good Matilda. I don't even have to hear your words to know what the story is about."

"Thanks," I blushed at his unexpected compliment.

He raised his eyebrows. "I just wish it really was Rad's head you got to hit with the frying pan. I'm sure his head is just as hard as the anvil."

I giggled and swallowed my food, remembering that he couldn't understand me with my mouth full.

"I've considered accidentally missing the anvil myself."

Twelve

I'D made up my mind to tell Trish and Bridget and Rad about my family. But during the next week, the perfect moment never came.

A few times I tried to be the go-between that Mrs. Shelley said I could be. But all my efforts fell flat.

I introduced Trish and Bridget to Rosemary and Biff at lunch one day. Trish mumbled something about being late for class and took off as fast as she could. Bridget stood uncertainly at our table. For a minute I thought she might sit down. But Trish yelled for her to follow, and off she went.

I suggested to Bridget that we help the girls in wheelchairs during P.E. one morning. She began pushing until we saw Trish, Rad, Barry, and Rick at the gym door. Suddenly she remembered something she'd left in the locker room and had to run back to get it.

Rad insisted I spend every minute in drama class with him. I said, "Why don't we go backstage and help David finish the sets?"

"No way I'm going near that looney," he snapped. "And you don't have time, anyway. We have to practice this scene again."

"What's wrong with you?" I snapped back. "We know this scene backward and forward. Even David knows it, and he's never read the script. I'm going back there to help whether you like it or not. Practice your lines with the mirror."

"Bravo!" Mr. Schmidt said in a stage whisper as I stomped up the steps past Trish.

"You're going to be very sorry. Every girl in school wants Rad, but he chose you." Trish's words stung. "You should be thrilled. I would be."

"But you have Barry," I said needlessly.

"I'd rather have Rad," she said.

"Do you ever think of anyone but yourself?" I asked her.

"If you thought more of yourself and your true friends and less of your crip buddies, you'd be much better off, Janet Martin."

I didn't even bother to correct my last name. I was too busy glaring at her. "I *am* paying attention to my true friends."

I turned and walked through the curtain, thankful that David wouldn't have heard the argument. His signed greeting was like a breath of fresh air. At that moment I understood exactly why he chose not to talk to people like Trish and Rad.

* * * * *

The day of the dress rehearsal for the play finally came. I didn't think it would ever be six o'clock. I'd been standing around in my costume since right after I got off the bus. Rosemary and Francis had helped me put my hair up on top of my head and had woven ribbons into the piled-up hair. We were all in our room waiting.

Tonight was the only dress rehearsal, just for the families. But I was a bundle of preperformance jitters even so.

Biff's knock on our door and announcement that it was time to go quieted my nerves a little. Now that the time had really come, I was beginning to calm down. I was ready for almost anything.

I lifted my long, flowing skirt and slowly strolled down the side hall into the kitchen.

"We have something for you before the play," James said.

One at a time, each of my brothers and sisters handed me a miniature rose from the greenhouse garden. Mom pinned them in my hair. Now I really looked like a princess.

"And so you don't get cold . . ." Mom took something off the back of the chair and handed it to me.

"A coat?" I asked in surprise as I ran my fingers over the soft wool I remembered from the first time we went shopping. "You made this for me?"

She gave me a hug. "I knew the minute I laid eyes on you that you would be one of us. And"—her eyes twinkled—"that you'd need a winter coat."

My eyes stung as Pop helped me on with my new coat. I felt tears threatening. Lately they were always right on the surface. "Thanks." It was all I could say.

"Come on, you guys." Biff started pushing us out the door. "All this mushy stuff will make Janet late for her starring role. And I want a front-row seat," Biff said.

When we got to school, that's where they sat, too. The Kingsley family filled the whole front row. I was no longer worried about my friends seeing them out there. The Kingsleys were my family, and I loved them.

I didn't have much time to think about that,

though. Rad was being impossible.

"Where is my cup for the first act?" he yelled at David.

"On the shelf marked '1st Act,' " David signed and I interpreted. The corners of his lips tipped slightly up. I knew he was secretly enjoying Rad's impatience while I translated.

"Just be sure it's out there when I need it," he shouted as he turned away.

David shrugged his shoulders. He couldn't read Rad's lips when he looked the other direction.

"Where are you going?" Rad yelled again. David must have picked up the loud sound on his hearing aids because he turned and waited for Rad to speak.

"What did you do with my skateboard? I laid it up against this wall when I came in. You've hidden it, haven't you?" He clenched his fists and walked stiffly over in front of David.

Calmly David reached for the pad in his pocket. I tried not to snicker as he wrote a few words on the paper and held it under Rad's nose. He pointed behind him to the skateboard. It stood on the wall where Rad had left it. But the mess Rad had made searching for his cup now covered the skateboard.

Rad yanked the board out from under the

scattered props and took off on it to the other side of the stage.

"That was cruel," I signed.

"He deserved it. He's been on my case for the last hour."

"We'd better get back to work. It would be a shame if I couldn't find that anvil."

David went back to organizing props and making sure the painted houses were set in order to be pulled out onto the stage for the village scene.

Before I knew what was happening, Rad flashed by on his skateboard, heading right for David. "Watch out," he warned as he made a big show of losing his balance and falling off the skateboard. The board rushed on without him and rammed into the back of David's ankles. The force and the surprise knocked him down.

"Gee, I'm awfully sorry," Rad mumbled. "I warned him. It's his fault he couldn't hear me!" Rad explained sweetly to the group that had gathered.

"No problem." David eyed him as he brushed himself off. He used his voice to get his point across this time. "Even the best have their falls."

This time it was Rad who was speechless.

The lights dimmed.

All the actors took their places onstage, waiting for the curtain to go up. I took a deep breath. I was so mad at Rad that it completely eliminated my stage-fright butterflies.

The lights came up with the curtain. I launched into the first scene like my life depended on it.

I gestured. I cried. I pleaded with Prince Marcus not to leave his poor, dear sister alone in the dark, dank castle. In real life, all I wanted was to kick him out the door.

How dare he fake an accident with that precious skateboard of his? The whole school knew he had never fallen off of it in his life.

"You were great out there," Bridget said to me during intermission. She lowered her eyes. "I saw what Rad did to David. It wasn't very nice."

"It wasn't an accident either," I told her angrily. "Rad's being a total jerk tonight. It's all I can do to be out there onstage with him."

Bridget touched my hand. "No matter what happens between you and Rad and even Trish for that matter, I was hoping we could still be friends," she told me. "Maybe," she added shyly, "I could eat lunch with you and your friends one day next week?"

I squeezed her hand. "Of course we can be

friends, Bridget. I'm not going to let Trish and Rad run my life anymore."

"She's not going to run my life anymore, either," Bridget said.

"In that case you're going to need some support. You're welcome to eat lunch with us anytime. Now let's go out there and knock 'em dead."

Bridget and I did our scene together and got laughs from the crowd in all the right places. Act by act the play wound down until the final clang of the anvil and the curtain calls.

Shouting and clapping louder than anyone else was the whole front row of Kingsleys. The curtain closed and opened again at the insistence of the audience.

The cast bowed, and Mr. Schmidt brought out David and the other backstage hands, too.

After the last bow, we got a standing ovation from an obviously biased audience. Mr. Schmidt left the curtain open, and the parents all came up onstage to congratulate their kids.

The Kingsleys stayed on the lower floor, since they couldn't get James' wheelchair up the steep steps.

"Who invited them?" Rad asked with a sneer.

I sidestepped him as he tried to put his arm around me.

Trish was right there to back him up. "Yeah, dress rehearsal was supposed to be just for relatives."

"They came to watch me," I said happily.

Suddenly the stage grew quiet. Everyone had quieted down and was listening to our conversation.

"What have you done? Adopted every crip in school?" Rad chuckled at his own joke. His laughter bounced off the silent crowd and echoed around the stage.

I handed Rad an extra copy of the play program. I pointed out the section where my new name, Janet Kingsley, was printed in bold black ink.

"Nope." I read my name out loud. "They adopted me!"

Someone started clapping. I think it was Bridget or maybe Mr. Schmidt. Soon everyone was clapping and shouting congratulations. Everyone except Rad and Trish. Maybe there was hope for this school after all.

I took David's outstretched hand. Then I followed him down the stairs to the waiting arms of my family—the family I wouldn't leave "no matter what."

About the Author

CINDY SAVAGE lives in a big rambling house on a tiny farm in northern California with her husband, Greg, her three birth children, and an assortment of foster children.

She published her first poem in a local newspaper when she was six years old, and soon got hooked on reading and writing. After college she taught bilingual Spanish/English preschool, then took a break to have her own children. Now she stays home with her kids and writes magazine articles and books for children and young adults.

In between writing and acting as chauffeur to a very active family, she reads, does needlework, bakes bread, and tends the garden.

Traveling has always been one of her favorite hobbies. As a child she crossed the United States many times with her parents, visiting Canada and Mexico along the way. Now she takes shorter trips to the ocean and the mountains to get recharged. She gets her inspiration to write from the places she visits and the people she meets.